Holiday Princess

A Princess Diaries Book

MEG CABOT

Holiday Princess

Illustrated by Chesley McLaren

■ HARPERCOLLINS*PUBLISHERS*

Holiday Princess:

A Princess Diaries Book

Text copyright © 2005 by Meggin Cabot

Illustrations copyright © 2005 by HarperCollins Publishers Inc.
All rights reserved. No part of this book may be used or repro-
duced in any manner whatsoever without written permission except
in the case of brief quotations embodied in critical articles and
reviews. Printed in the United States of America. For information
address HarperCollins Children's Books, a division of
HarperCollins Publishers, 1350 Avenue of the Americas, New
York, NY 10019.

www.harperteen.com

Library of Congress Cataloging-in-Publication Data
Cabot, Meg.
  Holiday princess / Meg Cabot ; illustrated by Chesley
McLaren.—1st ed.
    p.   cm. — (A princess diaries book)
  Summary: Princess Mia presents a guide to the winter holidays, including the story behind some traditions, gift suggestions,
makeup and fashion tips for seasonal parties, recipes, and craft
ideas.
  ISBN-10: 0-06-075434-6 — ISBN-13: 978-0-06-075434-1
  1. Holidays—Juvenile literature.   2. Winter festivals—Juvenile
literature.   3. Princesses—Juvenile literature. (1. Holidays.
2. Princesses) I. McLaren, Chesley, ill.   II. Title.   III. Series.
GT3933.C32 2005   2004028786
394.261—dc22

1 2 3 4 5 6 7 8 9 10
❖
First Edition

This book is for holiday princesses (and princes) everywhere

A royal thank-you to all who contributed to this book: Beth Ader, Jennifer Brown, Barb Cabot, Michele Jaffe, Laura Langlie, Abby McAden, Chesley McLaren, and especially royal consort Benjamin Egnatz.
—M.C.

Many thanks to Alison Donalty, Barbara Fitzsimmons, Sasha Illingworth, Abby McAden, and Meg Cabot for sharing the holiday princess spirit.
—C.M.

TABLE OF CONTENTS

Holiday Princess

INTRODUCTION

by Her Royal Highness Princess Mia Thermopolis

Sleigh Bells Ring

Sleigh bells ring! Are you listening? In the lane, snow is glistening. . . .

Well, okay, whatever, I've never actually heard sleigh bells. And there are no lanes in New York City, just streets and avenues (unless you count Minetta Lane down in the Village, which I don't because it smells like pee), and the snow never glistens here, it turns almost instantly into black slush because of all the car exhaust.

But that doesn't mean I don't wholeheartedly enjoy the holiday season when I get the chance. There's so much to do and see, sometimes I wonder how I'll ever get to it all.

That's why I, with the assistance of some of my friends and relatives, have composed this guide to help make what often turns out to be a hectic and stressful time more relaxed, so that we can all actually take the time to enjoy it. Because that's what the holiday season is all about—enjoying time with friends and family!

Holiday Etiquette

The holidays aren't just any other days . . . well, duh, since they're called holidays. But you get what I mean. They come laden with all this . . . stuff. Like, traditions.

And while some people, like my mom, believe traditions are for breaking, some other people, like Grandmère, believe traditions are the backbone of family and society and stuff.

I don't know who's right and who's wrong. Maybe they both are. All I know is, none of this has anything to do with presents. Which is a bummer, if you ask me.

HOLIDAY CARDS

by Grandmère, Dowager Princess of Genovia
[with commentary by Princess Mia in red, here and
throughout, wherever you see these brackets]

Sending Joy to Your Loved Ones for the Price of a Stamp

Cards sent during the holiday season are a lovely way to say
Joyeux Noël, Happy Hanukkah, or *Bonne Année* to a friend
or family member with whom you are not necessarily close
enough to exchange gifts, but who you nonetheless wish to
acknowledge.

The first Christmas card was sent by Sir Henry Cole,
an Englishman who, in 1843, wished to urge his friends not
to forget the needy during the holiday season. He commis-
sioned a small illustration of a happy family enjoying a succulent meal while failing to notice the destitute and squalid
conditions of the poor around them, and sent it to all of his
acquaintances.

[I totally applaud Sir Henry for the thought, but bummer
card to get in the mail!]

The tradition Sir Henry began soon caught on, and
sending illustrated cards at Christmas became the rage. It

is now a billion-dollar-a-year industry worldwide. It has become so widespread, in fact, with people sending so many cards to so many people, that they have managed to forget basic card etiquette. And that is that a card, however beautifully rendered, is not as important as the message written inside it. And by that I do not mean the message the card manufacturer has written inside it, but the message YOU, the SENDER, have written inside it.

Because the recipient of your card does not particularly

care if Hallmark wishes him or her a Happy New Year. What the recipient of your card cares about is YOU, and how YOU are doing.

That is why it is essential to HANDWRITE a short note in each and every card you send, no matter how many cards that may be. The Palais Royal de Genovia sends out more than one thousand cards per year, and I personally handwrite messages on each one, such as:

> *Dearest Charles,*
> *I do hope you and Camilla will drop*
> *in during your next trip to Biarritz.*
> *Merry Christmas, and the happiest of*
> *New Years to you and your children.*
> *Much love,*
> *Clarisse*

This is perfectly adequate. It is, of course, ultimately the thought that counts.

This does not mean, however, that this horrid American tradition of sending photocopied "Christmas newsletters" is acceptable! Far from it. I can understand persons with children wishing to let friends and family know of their progeny's progress in school or games. And, therefore, I will allow that a one-page note of this kind, WITH A PERSONAL MESSAGE HANDWRITTEN ACROSS THE TOP, ENCLOSED IN A TASTEFUL CARD, is permissible.

What I cannot condone are the two-, three-, or even FOUR-page single-spaced NOVELS people seem to feel compelled to send today. I do not particularly care to know the details about "Grandmum's" latest knee surgery, or the final score of every single one of "Harry's" polo matches. Careful selection of the year's highlights, related in a fairly HUMOROUS manner, is the only way letters of this kind can succeed.

Since it seems highly unlikely, however, that anyone is ever going to follow my advice, I can only hope the holiday newsletter goes the way of bell-bottoms, and fades from view.

[Uh, Grandmère? Bell-bottoms are back in style now. And I personally LOVE getting Christmas newsletters, the longer the better. My favorite is the one Mr. Gianini's sister sends out every year listing her kids'—Nathan and Claire— many many social and athletic accomplishments. For instance, Nathan was voted Heaviest Sleeper at his sleep-away camp last summer. And Claire graduated from the Barbizon School of Modeling with top honors, particularly in Runway Walking and Product Endorsement. It warms my heart each holiday season to know that Nathan and Claire? Yeah, they're just keepin' it real.]

IT'S NOT JUST ABOUT GIFTS—
PLUS, A SNIP 'N' SAVE GIFT LIST!

by Princess Mia

Everyone knows that Christmas is the celebration of the birth of Jesus Christ, who was born about two thousand years ago. The funny thing is, no one really knows whether Jesus was REALLY born on December 25. In fact, he probably wasn't, and this date was chosen because of the popular ancient Persian god, Mithras, who was also supposedly born on this day.

But who cares? It's still a totally fun holiday—especially when combined with all that Santa stuff . . . not to mention the excellent food! It would be wrong to assume that vegetarians such as myself can't have a delicious holiday meal. True, it isn't easy, considering all the poor fowl that are forced to give up their lives every December 25th.

But, as I've trained my mother, and even my grandmother, it is perfectly possible to have a sumptuous meal during the holidays for which not one animal had to give its life. There's cranberry bread, of course (you don't even need eggs to make it, though I don't count eggs as animals if they don't contain baby chicks . . . and I do eat fish because, well, you can't pet them, and they don't have much personality anyway, and besides, I really like sushi), and delicious broccoli soup and roasted Brussels sprouts and garlic mashed potatoes and pumpkin pie and apple relish . . . well, I could go on and on. But most importantly, of course, there's PRESENTS.

Some historians say we give presents at Christmastime because that's what the ancient Romans used to do at Saturnalia, a winter solstice celebration. Others say we give presents because of the gifts the Three Wise Men brought to baby Jesus. Still others say we give gifts in memory of St. Nicholas, who was a really generous guy.

I say: Who cares WHY we give gifts? Just keep 'em coming.

Oh yeah: It's important to GIVE. Otherwise, you won't RECEIVE.

HANDY SNIP 'N' SAVE ROYAL GENOVIAN GIFT LIST:

For	Gift Idea
Mom	
Dad	
Stepparents	
Siblings	
Best friend	
Other friends	
Boyfriend	
Grandparents	

Uncles, aunts, cousins	
Pet	
Biology lab partner	
Teachers	
Postal carrier	
Newspaper deliverer	
Favorite Chinese food deliveryperson	
Bodyguard	
Royal chauffeur	
Personal maid	
Others	

To:

Love: Me

GIFTS FOR GUYS

by Tina Hakim Baba, romance expert

Just Say No to Expensive Electronics

Let's face it. Guys are IMPOSSIBLE to shop for. The only person harder to shop for than your dad is your boyfriend, and that's because your boyfriend's gift has to be imbued with all this meaning and stuff. Otherwise, it's like, what's the point?

Hopefully you and your guy have some private jokes or at least shared musical taste. That way you can always get him a joke present—like, if you two are obsessed with the violinist Joshua Bell, you could get him an autographed 8x11 of Joshua Bell—or a CD he's been dying to hear.

But let's say your private jokes are about something that can't be bought in a store, purchased from a fan club, or even handmade, and a CD just won't cut it. What's a lovelorn girl to do?

Follow these simple steps, and the hearth glow of your love will never die.

Gifts for the Guy You Aren't Dating, But Hope to Be Someday:
FOOD. The way to a man's (or woman's) heart is through the stomach. You can never go wrong with gifts of homemade

cookies, candy, or fudge (homemade cheese balls make excellent gifts for people on low-carb or sugar-free diets). Just make sure your guy doesn't have any food allergies—if he does, do not prepare him anything containing that substance.

Food gifts are appropriate for ANY guy of ANY duration of acquaintance. They are ALWAYS welcome. Whether it's the hot guy who works out next to you at the gym, your lab partner, or just the cute guy you see sometimes at the bus stop, just fork over a prettily wrapped tin of whatever, say, "I made this for you. Happy holidays!" and he'll be blushing to his hairline.

[To avoid teasing/rumors, you might want to give similarly wrapped tins to friends, so he doesn't think he's the ONLY one who got one, and that you're a creepy stalker he should run from like a startled fawn.]

Gifts for the Guy You've Only Been Out with Once or Twice on Group Dates: Food is also an excellent gift for this person, but you could move up a smidge on the intimacy scale and give him something else handmade, such as mittens if you knit, or a CD mix you burned yourself. A book or DVD might also be appropriate. Expensive jewelry or clothing is NOT acceptable for this person. He hasn't professed his undying love for you, and so does not deserve to be showered with electronics or gold at this point in the relationship.

Gifts for the Guy You're Dating Exclusively:
This is the hardest person of all to shop for—or the easiest, depending. Again, gifts based on private jokes are always good. Food is good, but remember, he isn't going to gaze at an empty tin when he thinks of you the way he would at the stunning portrait you had your little brother take with your iCamera, presented in a beautiful homemade frame.

Whatever you do, do NOT spend an exorbitant sum on a gift for your romantic partner. Christmas, Hanukkah, and Kwanzaa gifts are supposed to be MEANINGFUL, not expensive. Do NOT buy him a gold ID bracelet, for instance, because you're hoping he'll ask YOU to wear it. Do not buy him a leather jacket for the same reason, or a CD player (so NOT meaningful) or car stereo. You want to make sure he's staying with you for YOU, not your money.

This is why the best gift for your one true love is ALWAYS a kiss accompanied by something you made yourself, be it food, a CD, or a lovely hand-knitted steering wheel cover.

[I could not agree more.]

HOLIDAY PARTY LOOKS

by Paolo, royal hair stylist and cosmetician

If We Took a Holiday/Took Some Time to Celebrate

I am Paolo, beauty advisor to the Princess Amelia. Many will say the holiday season is, for women, a time to break out the green velvet dress with the red satin sash, and those shiny patent leather Mary Janes. . . .

Well, not I! I spit on green velvet! I say the holiday season is a time to break free and take a risk! Wear black instead of red to the company Christmas party. Trade in that light-up Santa pin for a studded leather bracelet. Get rid of reindeer sweater. Listen to Paolo: NO MORE REINDEER SWEATER!

Holiday time is the time to try new things. Put on those false sparkle eyelashes you've been wanting to try. Yes! Wear them to school! Who cares what the people say? The people know nothing! You want to wear the plaid pants? Wear them! Never will you have a better chance to take the fashion risk than during the holiday season, when you can blame a fashion faux pas on the Christmas spirit!

[Truer words were never spoken. I tried out my Christmas-Ornaments-as-Earrings Scheme and it went over like a

charm. Until Principal Gupta saw them and made me take them out. Who knew Rudolph and Frosty weren't part of Albert Einstein High's regulation school uniform?]

{*Princess Party Tip:*
To apply false eyelashes, first:

Make up your eyes in your normal fashion (shadow, liner, mascara). You will have a hard time applying these things AFTER the lashes are glued on.

Next, TRIM the lashes to fit the width of your eyes. False eyelashes are NOT one size fits all.

Then apply to the lashes a SMALL amount of the glue that came with the lashes (remember, you are putting glue

NEAR YOUR EYE. USE ONLY SPECIALLY DESIGNED FALSE EYELASH GLUE FOR THIS) and, with tweezers or clean fingers, apply lashes to upper lid, making sure to tamp them down so that they rest against your real eyelashes.

Don't expect to execute the above move in one try. It will take LOTS of practice before you get it right.

Once you've gotten it right, and after the glue has dried, gently CURL your lashes with your eyelash curler so the fake ones blend better with your real lashes, then apply another layer of mascara. Blink a few times to make sure the fake lashes stay in place.

You're good to go!
Enjoy!}

HOLIDAY GIFT WRAP

*by Sebastiano, royal fashion designer
and wardrobe consultant*

You CAN Judge a Gift by Its Cover

You do not need to spend a fort* this hol* seas* on exp*
gift wrap* paper! You can make your own! Is EASY! Just
fol* these sim* steps!

[Sebastiano still has trouble grasping basic English, as it is
a second language for him. What he means is, "You don't
need to spend a fortune this holiday season on expensive gift
wrapping paper. Just follow these simple steps." Here, why
don't I just translate the rest:

You will need:
- Butcher paper (available in any art store)*
- Scissors
- Acrylic paint
- Paint brushes
- Tape

Cut out the desired amount of butcher paper needed to cover the gift. Using the acrylic paint and your imagination, paint colorful designs or messages all over one side of the paper (Important: paint just ONE side of the paper). After the paint is fully dry, wrap your present, using tape to hold it in place.

Beautiful and personal!

You may want to use raffia (available at any plant or craft store) as ribbon.

*You can also use newspaper and pages torn from magazines for a more colorful or collage-y effect.]

See? Beaut*!

[*Beautiful.]

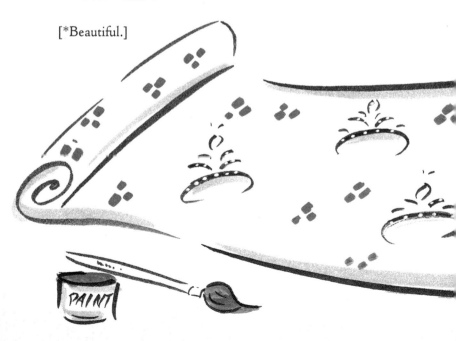

II

Hanukkah Lights

A Note from
Her Royal Highness Princess Mia

Hanukkah, or the Feast of the Dedication, is an ancient Jewish celebration, in which everyone gets a lot more presents than I do, which is not fair.

Also, everyone gets to eat latkes, which are potato pancakes that you dip in applesauce . . . not to be confused with scallion pancakes from Number One Noodle Son, which you dip in soy sauce. But just as tasty, actually.

GO TEAM MACCABEE

by Michael Moscovitz,
Royal Consort to the Princess of Genovia

Contrary to popular opinion, Hanukkah isn't about getting eight presents on eight consecutive nights. Well, I mean, that happens. But that's not what it's about.

Hanukkah is actually a celebration dating back two thousand years, when in Palestine, Antiochus the Syrian, a guy who hated everybody and vowed to destroy all faiths but his own, was killed by the Maccabees, led by Judah.

Everyone was psyched that Antiochus was finally dead, and ready to get back to their normal routine. But when Judah went to light the eternal flame in the Temple lamp, there was only a small container of sacred oil left—just about enough for a single night, which was a huge deal, because in order to reconsecrate the Temple, which Antiochus had basically trashed, they had to have the eternal flame going . . . and it was going to take eight days to make new oil.

Which meant, basically, that Judah was screwed.

So you can imagine his surprise—not to mention everyone else's—when that one little container of oil miraculously lasted throughout the eight days it took to get the new oil. It's this miracle that Jews celebrate during the eight nights of Hanukkah, when we gather in our homes to light the eight candles in the Hanukkah lamp (aka, the menorah).

[Don't forget the presents.]

Traditionally, on the eight nights of Hanukkah, children are given gifts.

[Eight gifts. One for every night. Which is way more than I ever get at Christmas. Not that it's about the gifts, of course.]

Another one of the best known symbols of Hanukkah is the dreidel. Although the dreidel (the origins of which go back to a game called "totum" or "teetotum," which was played in England and Ireland in the sixteenth century) has long been associated with Hanukkah and children, the story behind the dreidel is actually super serious: In times when Jews were forbidden to meet and practice their religious beliefs, men would keep a dreidel and gelt (money) handy while gathering to study the Torah (the Hebrew bible). When soldiers would approach, the men would pull out the dreidel and pretend to be playing a game. So basically, the dreidel saved their lives.

[And this is where we get the famous "Dreidel Song":

Dreidel dreidel dreidel
I made it out of clay
And when it's dry and ready
Then dreidel I will play.

Not to be confused with the other famous Hanukkah song by Adam Sandler.]

{*Princess Party Tip:*
Forget Spin the Bottle! At your next party, play Spin the Dreidel! Players can use coins, candy, nuts, raisins, or chocolate coins (gelt) as tokens or chips. To play the game, a player spins the dreidel. When the dreidel stops, the letter that is facing up decides the player's fate:

NUN: nothing happens—next player spins the dreidel
GIMEL: player takes all tokens in the pot
HEH: player takes half of the pot
SHIN: player must put one token into the pot

NUN נ
GIMEL ג
HEH ה
SHIN ש

(Together these letters stand for the phrase "Nes gadol hayah sham," which means "A great miracle happened there." In Israel the dreidel is a bit different in that their letters stand for "A great miracle happened here.")

You can also play the dreidel MY way: Whoever the dreidel points at after it lands is the person the spinner has to kiss.

Enjoy!}

III

Yuletide Past & Present

Did you ever wonder where all these crazy holiday traditions come from? My mom says they all come from Mamaw, her mother, back in Versailles, Indiana, and that's why we must rebel against them with all of our might.

But my mom's not actually right about that—the Mamaw part, I mean. Most of the holiday traditions we participate in today actually got their start way, way before Mamaw was ever born.

Although you might not believe it, to look at her.

Mamaw, I mean. Especially when she's not wearing her bridge.

A BRIEF HISTORY OF THE SOLSTICE— OUR PAGAN PAST

by Lilly Moscovitz, creator, writer, director, and host of Lilly Tells It Like It Is

So, let's face it: Winter sucks.

Oh, sure, there's the ice skating and hot chocolate and the Nondenominational Winter Dance and stuff.

But there didn't used to be. A long time ago, back in what they call pagan times, before they had mini-marshmallows or Times Square or even electricity, people used to get really bummed out around December 21. That's because December 21 was (and still is) the shortest day of the year, also known as the winter solstice (the solstice is when the sun is at its greatest distance from the celestial equator, which means farthest away from Earth).

[On the solstice, you can supposedly balance an egg on its end and it will stay like that. Because of the magnetic forces. Try it, it works . . . if you practice enough.]

Anyway, for ancient people who worshiped the sun and all of that, the winter solstice truly sucked, because they feared that the gods had forsaken them, since the days were getting shorter (you would think, considering this happened

EVERY year, they'd have caught on sooner or later. But whatever). They got all scared life on Earth as they knew it would end if the gods didn't let the sun shine again.

So the ancients did what any of us would do when we're feeling bummed:

They partied.

Seriously. They built these big fires to encourage the sun to shine again, and then, when it worked (because, um, it always worked), they'd party with these giant feasts and stuff, because they all realized spring was coming and they weren't all going to die after all.

Some of these ancient parties included:

- Feast of Aset: The Egyptians, who were big partiers, held a winter festival that honored Isis, mother of the sun god Horus. It probably wasn't a good idea to be around during the Feast of Aset if you were a virgin. Or a sheep.

- Saturnalia: The Romans paid homage to Saturn, the god of agriculture, with this festival. People pranced around with garlands on their heads, giving candles and green wreaths as presents. And, knowing the ancient Romans, there was probably some throwing up as well.

- Feast of Mithras: To the Persians (where Iran is today), December 25 was Unconquered Sun (Mithras) Day. They were so successful in promoting this belief that it even spread to ancient Britain, until King Arthur was all, ENOUGH already, and ran around cutting off people's heads with the help of Keira Knightley in her leather bikini.

- Yule: The Norsemen started this big feast called "Jiuleis" or "Giulu," later shortened to just plain "Yule." Beginning on December 20 or 21, Yule spanned twelve days, ending on "Yule Night," or December 31 (this is where the twelve days of Christmas come from. Although I highly doubt these guys messed around with any partridges, except to eat them). These dudes would kill a bunch of cows when the grasses died out and roast them over a Yule log, which was lit from a piece of the previous year's Yule log that had been saved (actually, the whole Christmas tree thing that we enjoy today is an extension of Yule, since it was thought that the sacrifice of a great tree would insure that life would go on in spite of the cold and bad weather).

Wiccans still celebrate Yule as the first of the solar festivals and the first Sabbath of the new year, doing stuff like caroling and wassailing.

[I love *Charmed,* even though they've never actually shown Alyssa Milano wassailing. I would love it even more if they DID show this.]

However these ancient midwinter feasts and festivals were carried out—from Mithras to Saturnalia—they all had one thing in common: They were parties to celebrate the victory of light and life over darkness, and a time of hope born anew.

[Also the time for the getting of presents. Such as the Segway Human Transporter I've been wanting for a VERY long time.]

{*Princess Party Tip:*
Holiday Wassail
   You can have your own little Wiccan Yule celebration by simmering the following on a stove:

- 1 gallon apple cider
- 25–30 whole cloves
- 6–10 cinnamon sticks
- 1 quart pineapple juice
- One 6-ounce can frozen orange juice concentrate
  Serves 8–10

Sounds a lot like hot apple cider, doesn't it? Well, it's not. It's wassail!}

HOLLY AND MISTLETOE

by Frank Gianini,
Algebra teacher and stepfather of Princess Mia

Druid's Delite

Okay, so, holly comes from this bush, see, and was traditionally the sacred plant of Saturn, and so it was very popular at the ancient Roman Saturnalia festival around solstice time (December 21), where everybody traditionally got down and drank a lot. Like a Grateful Dead concert, only no Jerry Garcia. Romans used to give one another holly wreaths during Saturnalia, to decorate the house with . . . kind of the way Deadheads do with tie-dye stuff.

A bunch of centuries later, in December, while the Romans continued doing their pagan thing, Christians celebrated the birth of Jesus. Only to avoid getting found out—you know, that they weren't into Saturn, like everybody else—they decorated their homes with Saturnalia holly.

[Just like the song "Ring around the Rosy" turns out to be about the plague, the song "Deck the Halls" turns out to be about avoiding religious persecution through subterfuge. Who knew?]

As there got to be more and more Christians, and their customs got more popular, holly lost its pagan association and became a symbol of Christmas. Get it?

Mistletoe. Okay, mistletoe is basically a weed that has no roots of its own. Instead, it lives off the tree that it attaches itself to, like a leech. Or like Yoko Ono.

Still, in ancient times, mistletoe was thought to have these miraculous healing properties (like another weed we all know), as well as bringing good luck to whoever stood under a sprig of it. Eventually this evolved to whoever stood under it while getting kissed by whoever was standing nearby.

{*Princess Party Tip:*
Real mistletoe in short supply? Make your own! All you need is
↼ Green felt
↼ White imitation pearls
↼ Scissors
↼ Glue

Cut out two leaf shapes from the green felt. Glue them together. In the middle of where they are joined, glue several imitation pearls. Let dry. Then hold your fake mistletoe over your head when a cute guy approaches, and tell him he has to kiss you.

It works!
Enjoy!}

IV

Christmas Around the World.

It's easy to think, when you're caught up in the holiday hordes on the subway, trying to get home after a brutal day at the Tiffany's gift counter (where all you wanted to buy was a crystal apple for your French teacher, Mademoiselle Klein, but this lady from New Jersey who was buying a key chain shaped like a golf bag kept cutting in front of you until finally you had to be all, "LADY! I WAS HERE FIRST!"), that this is what Christmas is like around the world . . . the snow, the angry taxi drivers, the tourists asking you where they can find Green-Witch Village.

But the truth is, Christmas is celebrated in VERY different ways outside of New York . . . and even outside of America. Who knew not everyone watches the burning Yule log on Channel Eleven Christmas morning?

Not me.

CHRISTMAS IN NYC

by Lilly Moscovitz, independent Christmas observer

TV and Chinese Food, Baby

Even though I am Jewish, I can tell you all about Christmas in New York. In fact, I am probably in a BETTER position to tell you about Christmas in New York than anyone, as I am unbiased toward the season, and more of an independent observer of the whole thing.

The Christmas season in New York City officially begins the day after Thanksgiving, also commonly referred to by the retail industry as Black Friday. This is because the day after Thanksgiving, which many New Yorkers have off, is when most people begin their Christmas shopping. It is usually the busiest shopping day of the year (followed by December 26, on which everyone exchanges the things they received that were bought the day after Thanksgiving).

It is around this time that department stores in New York City unveil their Christmas window displays. Many New Yorkers—not to mention tourists visiting the city—take an afternoon to walk around and admire these displays, which can contain animatronic puppets, music (actually piped outside through loudspeakers), and even live actors, though sadly none you'd actually want to see. Generally these displays are reviewed in the newspaper, and those declared most creative become the most popular, and are a source of pride for the store.

On December 1 or thereabouts, a giant tree is put up in Rockefeller Center (next to Prometheus, the big gold man statue that guards the ice skating rink). A committee is formed every year to scour the country for the biggest, nicest tree in the land, and then whoever owns it is asked to donate it to the city. Usually people are so honored they say yes. This is when Mia usually starts complaining about what a mean thing that is to do to a nice old tree.

Then the tree is decorated, and a few days later, in a solemn ceremony featuring performances from many fine artists (note sarcasm) like Mariah Carey or Celine Dion, the tree is lit by the mayor or some other dignitary, such as Mia Thermopolis. This usually indicates to New Yorkers that they have only a few weeks left to finish their Christmas shopping, and thus throws them into a rabid frenzy of shopaholism, so that they're in a worse mood than ever. Also around this time, the first snowfall of the year will occur, causing huge traffic headaches and making it impossible to find a parking place.

After this, it's just a matter of getting your shopping done, and getting all of your Christmas Eve

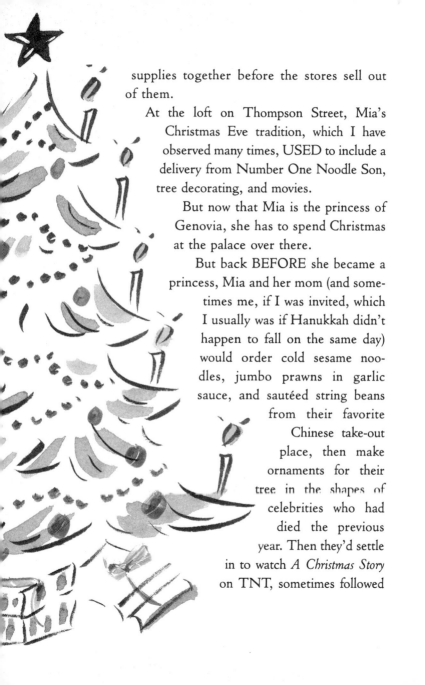

supplies together before the stores sell out of them.

At the loft on Thompson Street, Mia's Christmas Eve tradition, which I have observed many times, USED to include a delivery from Number One Noodle Son, tree decorating, and movies.

But now that Mia is the princess of Genovia, she has to spend Christmas at the palace over there.

But back BEFORE she became a princess, Mia and her mom (and sometimes me, if I was invited, which I usually was if Hanukkah didn't happen to fall on the same day) would order cold sesame noodles, jumbo prawns in garlic sauce, and sautéed string beans from their favorite Chinese take-out place, then make ornaments for their tree in the shapes of celebrities who had died the previous year. Then they'd settle in to watch *A Christmas Story* on TNT, sometimes followed by *Home for the Holidays* or *The Ref*, their other two favorite holiday movies.

Christmas morning, after sleeping in, Mia and her mom would have Christmas pancakes (pancakes in the shape of Christmas trees, an invention of Mia's mom) and open presents. Sometimes Mia's mom's friends would stop by (now Mr. Gianini's parents come over, to see the baby). Mia would usually never stick around for this, though, and would instead head on over to MY apartment to show off whatever presents she'd gotten, and hope for a glimpse of my brother's naked chest as he emerged from the shower or whatever (though she doesn't know I know this. Also, GROSS.).

In many parts of the country, shops and theaters are closed on Christmas Day. Not in New York. That's because there's such a large, multicultural community here, not everyone celebrates Christmas. So you can go to any restaurant, most shops, and any movie theater, just like on a regular day. Mia used to join us on a trip to the movies and then to Chinatown for dim sum on Christmas Day.

That is, until she became princess of Genovia and was forced to spend all of her holidays in Genovia. Where there is no Chinatown. Or dim sum. Or snow.

I'm telling you, Christmas in New York can't be beat.

[I can't believe she knew about my spying on Michael the WHOLE TIME!!!!!!!!!!!!!!]

CHRISTMAS IN GENOVIA

by Grandmère, Dowager Princess of Genovia

The Perfect Holiday

Christmas is a magical time in the small European principality of Genovia. Shopkeepers dress their windows with only the most tasteful of holiday displays, and the sound of church bells ringing in Advent fills the ears and warms the heart.

[Those stupid bells are so loud, they wake me up at the crack of dawn. I don't know how anybody is supposed to be filled with the Christmas spirit with only, like, five hours of sleep.]

The bustling marketplace is filled with succulent treats of the season, such as figs, truffles, tangerines, and smoked fish. In the *pâtisserie*, beautiful *bûches de Noël* are on display, with intricate decorations made from meringue. And everywhere can be heard the happy cries of "Joyeux Noël!" from the townsfolk.

[I seriously don't know what Grandmère is talking about. All I ever hear when I go down into the marketplace is people saying, "Get out of my way!" and "Move!", so they can get their Christmas shopping over with and get home in time for *Baywatch*.]

Christmas Eve is, of course, one of the most exciting nights of the year in Genovia. It's when the tree in the Palais Royal is unveiled, in all of its bejeweled glory, for the first time. Champagne flows, and one can feel a frisson of festivity in the air!

[I think Grandmère is mistaking the fumes from her cigarettes for frisson. That's the only thing *I've* ever noticed in the air on Christmas Eve.]

It is Genovian tradition to eat a humble repast the night before Christmas, and so a meager supper of lobster bisque, mussels in white wine sauce, brandade, various salads and breads, and assorted cheeses and fruits followed by meringue, is consumed before everyone heads off to midnight mass in the chapel. Nothing could be more beautiful than hearing the Royal Genovian Choir raise their voices in a jubilant rendition of "Adeste Fidelis."

["Oh Come All Ye Faithful" in English.]

After mass, everyone returns to the palace and to bed, to be awakened in the morning by the joyous ringing of church bells.

[Yeah. At eight in the morning. After having been at church until one. I always feel joyous about that, all right.]

Then everyone gathers for a delicious champagne breakfast of omelets and beignets, while gifts brought during the night by Père Noël are opened. The happy cries of the village children as they find their Christmas dreams coming true can be heard through the French doors, left open to let in the warm sea breeze and gentle Mediterranean sunlight.

[Unless my dad has a hangover, which he usually does. Then he makes Grandmère shut the French doors because the Mediterranean sunlight doesn't feel so gentle to HIM.]

After the last gift has been unwrapped, we head to the Genovian hospital and orphanage to bring gifts of candy and toys to those in need. Because, after all, that's what the holiday season is all about—giving to those less fortunate than yourself. God bless us, everyone!

[Oh, brother!]

CHRISTMAS IN INDIANA

by Hank Thermopolis, underwear model and Hoosier

I Wasn't the One Who Shot That Horse

Princess Mia asked me to jaw about Christmas in my hometown of Versailles, Indiana, and I said I'd be right pleased to.

Christmas is a BIG DEAL in Versailles. First off, Mamaw and Papaw—they raised me from a baby on account of my real mom, Mia's mom's sister, living on that commune—start putting up the Christmas decorations at the Handy Dandy Hardware Store just after Halloween. Some folks complain that they shouldn't be up before Thanksgiving, but Mamaw says they're just Christmas-Hating Scrooges.

New Yorkers may think they're fancy with their big tree at Rockefeller Center, but in Versailles we got our own tradition: We string pretty lights up all around the courthouse, and turn them on December 1. You should see 'em twinkle! For a while you could take a carriage ride around the square under the lights at night, until Jim Waddell and some of his friends (I didn't have nothing to do with it, despite what some folks might believe) took to shooting at the horses with their BB guns and frightened one so bad it took off down the street. Unfortunately for Jim, the mayor and his wife and kids were inside the carriage Old Gray was pulling at the time.

After that, the mayor said no more carriage rides. Also, Jim went to jail. Old Gray was fine though, don't you worry.

Christmas Eve at Mamaw and Papaw's, it's traditional to decorate the tree (a real one Papaw and me cut down from Musgrove Orchard and tie to the roof of the car real fast before Old Man Musgrove can catch us) and drink eggnog while listening to Mamaw's favorite Christmas record, Reba McEntire's "Fancy" ("I might have been born just plain white trash, but Fancy was my name"). Usually everyone we know stops by for some nog, and Mamaw fries up some funnel cakes. Then we watch *Grandma Got Run Over by a Reindeer* or *Ernest Saves Christmas*, and hit the hay, since Santa's on his way!

Christmas morning, we have to wake up bright and early in order to get to all those presents. We open 'em up, while Mamaw whips up some biscuits and gravy and country-fried ham. Then we change into our Sunday best and head over to church. Usually there's a Christmas pageant with real live sheep, and one of 'em almost always gets away. So me and Terry Pritchard have to spend most of the sermon chasin' it. After church, it's back home to change into our civvies and head on over to the shooting range to show off whatever gun Santa brought us.

And that's a real Hoosier Christmas!

[I am speechless.]

CHRISTMAS AROUND THE WORLD

by Princess Mia

One Crazy Night, Dozens of Ways to Celebrate It

Christmas is celebrated in many ways throughout the world. Not everyone celebrates American style, with a big turkey, or British style, with a plum pudding, and Santa doesn't actually visit EVERY country in the world.

If you happen to be royalty, like me, it's important to know how cultures other than your own celebrate their special days, or you could make a really big ass out of yourself at some regal function.

Read on to find out how Christmas is enjoyed in other parts of the world:

Australia

Christmas Down Under takes place in the heat of summer, since Australia is located in the southern hemisphere! So some Australians get to have their Christmas dinner on the beach. Which is totally unfair. Palm trees and surfing, at Christmastime? Lucky Australians—they get Father Christmas and summer breeze at the same time!

Austria

One would expect that at holiday time, the home country of the Trapp Family Singers would be all about music, and it is. What else would you expect from the birthplace of Wolfgang Amadeus Mozart, Johann Strauss Sr., and Jr., and Franz Schubert? You'll find concerts galore in Austria come Christmastime, along with visits from St. Nicholas on December 6, and the Christkindl (Christ Child) Christmas morning.

As an added bonus, Austrians celebrate December 5, also known as Krampus Day: Krampus is an evil spirit with a long red tongue and bulging eyes. On Krampus Day, it's traditional for children and adults to go together to the village to throw snowballs at Krampus, who is known to be Santa's mortal enemy. You heard it here first.

Belgium

Belgium, known throughout the world for its excellent *pommes frites* (aka French fries), is located between France and the Netherlands. In Belgium, St. Nick rides into town on a white horse or donkey. It's Father Christmas who's stuck with the reindeer.

Lucky Belgian kids, getting presents from TWO gift-giving dudes.

Brazil

Papai Noel (Father Noel) is the gift-bringer in Brazil. According to legend, he lives in Greenland, but when he arrives in Brazil, he strips down to his skivvies due to the summer heat. On December 25, most everybody goes to church, but the masses usually take place in the late afternoon, because everyone has to take a nap after their big *ceia de Natal*, Christmas dinner, which is held at midday, sometimes on the beach!

Canada

Canadians celebrate Christmas much like the rest of the North Americans do, except for the fact that Canadians observe Boxing Day, or the Feast of St. Stephen, on December 26. Supposedly on this day it was traditional for poor people to carry empty boxes from door to door, which the wealthier filled with food, money, and clothes they no longer wanted. Canadian parents are supposed to give their kids small gifts such as oranges, handkerchiefs, and socks on Boxing Day. Although I have never seen any record of this on *Degrassi*.

Chile

In Chile, Santa is known as El Viejo Pascuero, or Old Man Christmas. He looks like Santa Claus and he drives a team of reindeer, but since there aren't many chimneys in Chilean homes, due to the warm climate, El Viejo Pascuero climbs through the window with his gifts.

He better not try this in New York City, or he might run into a little trouble!

Colombia

Colombians take the holiday season super seriously! A traditional Colombian Christmas dinner would include *ajiaco*, a soup with potatoes and chicken, *natilla*, a corn-based dessert, and pastries called *buñuelos*. Traditionally, El Niño Jesús, the Christ Child, is the one who brings kids their gifts, not Santa. Christmas trees in Colombia are almost always fake, due to ecological reasons. Go Colombia, save those fir trees!

Cuba

Cuba is best known, of course, for the movie *Dirty Dancing: Havana Nights*. But it's also known for its hardcore Christmas celebrating. As in Spain, gifts are exchanged on the day of Epiphany, King's Day, on January 6. Children's gifts are brought by the Magi, or Reyes Magos. Even communism couldn't quell the Cubans' love for Christmas, and finally Fidel Castro, the reigning dictator, gave up trying. Take that, Señor Castro!

The Czech Republic

In the Czech Republic, the Christmas tree is lit on Christmas Eve after a huge meal that usually includes fish soup, salads, vegetables, potatoes, eggs, and carp (lots of countries eat fish and not meat on Christmas Eve). According to tradition, after dinner, a ringing bell indicates that the Christ Child has visited the home and has placed gifts under the tree for the kids in the house. When they hear the bell ring, all the kids run for it—kind of like Pavlov's dogs. An old Czech tradition involves placing a branch from a cherry tree in water, indoors, to bloom. If it flowers in time for Christmas, it's a sign that the winter may be short—kind of like our groundhog seeing (or not seeing) his shadow.

Denmark

Christmas is the most important event on the Danish calendar—in fact, this tiny nation consumes more candles per capita than any other country on Earth, mostly at Christmastime (I am sure the FDNY would have a thing or two to say about this). The Danish have a funny tradition involving an almond hidden in a bowl of rice pudding: whoever finds the almond gets a prize. Danish people also supposedly leave a bowl of the rice pudding out for the Julnisse—a mischievous elf who lives in the attic and plays jokes on people in the house. If he gets pudding, though, he will watch over the household throughout the year. This is sort of like Fat Louie, who gets very cranky when denied his Fancy Feast.

Dubai

Dubai, in the United Arab Emirates, is a multicultural society where it's not unusual to find people sunbathing on one of its many beaches on Christmas Day. In fact, it's a major vacation destination during the holidays. Shopping could almost be described as a national pastime in Dubai, since some Europeans actually make a special trip to this country to the many festively decorated markets just to do their Christmas shopping (Grandmère is one person I could mention who has been known to do this).

Estonia

In Estonia, most of the holiday action takes place on Christmas Eve. This is when the president of Estonia declares Christmas Peace. Declaring Christmas Peace is a 350-year-old tradition that began in the seventeenth century by order of Queen Kristina of Sweden. Go, Queen Kristina! The best known Christmas tradition in Estonia is mumming. Mummers are like mimes here in the U.S., only hopefully not as repulsive or annoying.

Finland

In Finland, home of the ice hotel, Christmas means family. Everyone comes home on Christmas Eve, even kids who have moved away and had kids of their own and swore they would never come back because they can't stand hearing about the Handy Dandy Hardware Store one more second. On Christmas Eve, Father Christmas comes to visit—but not down the chimney! In Finland, Father Christmas actually shows up while the kids are still awake, and asks them if they've been good. Only if they say yes do they get presents. I kind of doubt many say no.

France

On Christmas Eve, French children put their shoes, *sabots*, in front of the fireplace, instead of their stockings. But the hope is still the same—that Père Noël, Father Christmas, will fill their shoes with presents (hopefully they'll check to see first before putting their shoes on in the morning, because who wants to get caramel or whatever all over their socks?). Père Noël's partner, Père Fouettard, Father Spanker, "rewards" bad children with a spanking (France is so kinky!). The family Christmas dinner is followed by a *bûche de Noël*, a traditional French cake baked in the shape of a Yule log and decorated to look like one. Another famous cake served during the holiday season in France is a *galette des rois*, or king cake, served during the Feast of the Magi. A small figurine of a baby is baked inside the cake, and whichever children get the figurines are king and queen

for the day. This would never go over in the U.S., of course, due to the choking hazard.

Genovia

See "Christmas In Genovia," page 51.

Germany

German children are visited by St. Nicholas on December 6, when the old guy fills their shoes with candy if they've been good, or twigs if they've been bad (ouch). In Germany, it's traditional to not let the children in the house to see the decorated tree until Christmas Eve. This would be very difficult to do in New York City, considering the size of the apartments here, but whatever. On Christmas Eve, everyone in

Germany eats a huge amount of white sausage and macaroni salad, followed on Christmas Day by another huge meal that includes *Christstollen*, fruit-and-nut-filled bread, and marzipan.

Then on December 26, everyone goes on Atkins in order to fit into their lederhosen again.

Greece

On Christmas Eve, Greek children go around their neighborhoods singing *kalanda*, or Greek carols. They're rewarded with candy by the appreciative Greek households for their efforts (presumably they don't have to take this candy to the local hospital to get it X-rayed for hidden razor blades before eating it the way my mom used to make me do on Halloween). The Christmas feast afterward is really important, since Christmas follows forty days of fasting for the Greek Orthodox Church, of which 95 percent of the population is a member. *Christopsomo*, Christ bread, is prepared for the meal, and throughout the twelve days of Christmas, a fire is kept burning in the fireplace to keep away the *kallikantzari*, elfin mischief-makers who make the milk sour. St. Nicholas, not Santa, comes calling on Greek children if they've been good.

Guatemala

For the nine days prior to Christmas, the streets in Guatemala are crawling with *las posadas* processions, reenactments of the search for shelter by Joseph and the pregnant Mary. On Christmas Eve at the stroke of midnight, the *abrazo de Navidad*, Christmas hug, takes place, not only within the family but also among friends and neighbors (I so would try not to be standing near Kenny at midnight if I were there). Christmas trees are popular, though usually they're artificial due to the climate. On Christmas morning, children wake to find gifts left under the tree by either the Christ Child or by Santa, depending on their family's religion. And only if they've been good, of course.

Hungary

The season starts early for Hungarians, with St. Nicholas visiting good Hungarian girls and boys on December 6. Next comes *Lucia Napja,* or St. Lucia's Day, on December 13, a time when bad spirits supposedly roam the land—and also when young girls can write down the names of boys they like, put them under their pillows, and draw out one name a day until Christmas Day—and that one will be the name of the guy she's destined to marry (I so wish we had this here in America. I am DYING to know if Michael will be my royal consort for life)!

Iceland

With a 99.9 percent literacy rate, you'd expect Iceland to have some cool customs, and they do. Icelandic Yule is all about family, with everyone pitching in to decorate for and celebrate St. Thorlakur's Day, named for Iceland's major native saint, Thorlakur Thorhallsson, former Bishop of Skálholt, on December 23. The main custom associated with Thorláksmessa (St. Thorlakur's Day) is eating skate (a fish. And, um, yuck). The Yule tree is usually decorated on this evening. The children in Iceland get not one, but thirteen Santas, known as Jólasveinar. They're supposed to be the tiny descendants of mythological figures known as Grýla the Ogre and Leppalúdi. Each one drops by with a gift, starting December 12, but the gifts can't be opened until Christmas Eve. Um, hello, thirteen gifts? I'm so moving to Iceland!!!!

Indonesia

Even though the majority of Indonesians are Muslims, there are still some parts of the nation that celebrate Christmas, with the season starting in some places as early as October (this is even earlier than the Grand Union puts up THEIR decorations! At least THEY wait until after Halloween). The season usually ends on the third Sunday of January with the Pigura Carnival, meaning "A Closing New Year Celebration," which is nicely to the point. Thanks, Indonesia.

Ireland

Despite what I have observed on St. Patrick's Day here in the U.S., Christmas in Ireland is generally more about religion than partying, with an important significance placed on the lighting of candles, especially in the window (to guide Santa's sleigh. Oh, and also friends who might want to visit), and with manger scenes in most homes (along with

Christmas trees, of course). St. Stephen's Day is celebrated in Ireland rather than Boxing Day, with pantomimes (plays) being the popular choice of entertainment. St. Stephen's Day also includes something called the Wren Boys' Procession, in which groups of young people go door to door in costumes, generally demanding pudding (dessert).

I would like to see them try to get away with this in the Bronx.

Israel

While it is a Jewish state, Israel IS home to Bethlehem, the birthplace of Christ. On December 25, people come from all over to visit the Church of the Nativity, which is said to have been built over what is considered to be the location of Christ's birth, with a fourteen-pointed silver star marking the location of the original manger. Visitors can attend Christmas Eve services there by invitation only, though the service is broadcast on huge television screens in what is known as Manger Square. Just like in Times Square on New Year's! Only with Jesus instead of Dick Clark!

Italy

Christmas in Italy is a combination of Christian tradition blended with the pagan practices of ancient Rome's winter solstice celebration, Saturnalia, which occurs at the same time as Advent. For instance, Christmas sweets containing nuts and honey are common throughout Italy (*panettone*, cake filled with candied fruit, and *torrone*, nougat), since in ancient Rome, honey was traditionally consumed around the solstice in hopes that the new year would be sweet, and nuts supposedly symbolize fertility (get it?). Though Santa, or Babbo Natale, comes to visit most Italian homes nowadays, traditionally the principal gift-bringer was an old lady named La Befana. But St. Lucia and Gesù Bambino (Baby Jesus) also bring presents. Lucky Italian kids, with all those people bringing them stuff! No wonder none of them ever wants to leave home.

Japan

While there's no official religious celebration of Christmas in Japan, as less than one percent of the population is Christian, many Japanese do celebrate it with a traditional Christmas cake and—less often—an artificial tree. Apparently, people in Japan are so into the Christmas cake deal, they can't believe we don't have Christmas cake here in the U.S. (at least, not in my house. We're lucky if anyone remembers to buy Christmas milk for my bowl of Christmas Froot Loops). December 25 is not a holiday from work, though, and New Year's Day is a much bigger deal to the Japanese. Kids still get presents, though, either from Santa Kurohsu or Hoteiosho, a god with eyes in the back of his head—so he really CAN see you sleeping. Or at least making faces at him behind his back.

Korea

Christmas is getting to be a bigger and bigger deal in Korea, with Christmas decorations going up in October and staying up sometimes until March. Just like in the U.S.!

Lithuania

Lithuanians love Christmas trees, and come December, almost every home has a decorated tree. *Prakartelis*—crèche or nativity scenes—are also popular with churches and schools. Lithuanian kids are lucky since they can get gifts on New Year's Day from Father Frost, Senis Saltis, and Father Christmas, Kaledu Senis, who come calling on Kucios, Christmas Eve. It's traditional on Christmas Eve in Lithuania for twelve special dishes to be served (representing the twelve months of the year), each containing no fat, milk, butter, or meat—the anti-Atkins! On Christmas Day, though, you can eat whatever you want in Lithuania.

Luxembourg

Christmas is celebrated in a fairly religious way in the tiny country of Luxembourg, with many families attending midnight mass. In addition, Santa Claus is said to still be a rarity in most homes, with the Christ Child bringing the Christmas gifts. The French *bûche de Noël* shows up in many Luxembourgian homes, along with a fruit-and-rum loaf called *stollen*, and black pudding or venison on Christmas Day. In case you didn't know, black pudding is made from congealed pig's blood. Just thought I'd share.

Mexico

Mexicans love Christmas, and are famous for their traditional reenactments of Joseph and Mary's search for a hotel room. They do this on nine consecutive nights before Christmas. The ritual of *las posadas* is a procession of children and adults that, as soon as it gets dark, heads through town until it gets to the house appointed to be the "inn" for that night, where the "innkeeper" invites the participants in for *colaciones*—candy—and, for the adults, plenty of tequila. This goes on for eight nights, but on Christmas Eve, the ninth evening, Baby Jesus joins the Holy Family in the *nacimiento*.

I sincerely hope there's a child safety seat on that donkey.

Monaco

The principality of Monaco, which borders Genovia, Italy, and France, has a Christmas tradition similar to the Genovian "rite of the olive branch," in that the youngest member of the family is required to soak an olive branch in a glass of grappa, then burn it while saying a bunch of nice things about olives, the country's main form of income (before cruise ships and baccarat came along). They still make the youngest member of the family (namely ME) do this in SOME countries I could mention.

Netherlands

In the Netherlands, St. Nicholas is known as Sinterklaas, and he shows up on his feast day, December 6, expecting to find the shoes of the children of the house filled with hay for his horse. If he does, he takes the hay out and fills the shoes with candy. If he doesn't, his assistant, Zwarte Piet, Black Pete, puts rocks or something equally unpleasant in the unfortunate child's shoe. Kleeschen is another Netherlandic name for St. Nicholas. Presents in the Netherlands are actually exchanged on December 5. So they have the whole rest of the month to exchange them for whatever they really wanted. Luckies.

New Zealand

In New Zealand, Santa rides into town on a fire engine, which if you ask me is an abuse of city-owned property. Many people in New Zealand barbecue on Christmas, but some still follow the old English traditions and have turkey and plum pudding—plus a pavlova, a sort of meringue. Some New Zealanders celebrate two Christmases—the second one in July, which is winter for them, complete with a tree. In some homes, a traditional Maori *hangi* is built outside. This is like a Hawaiian luau, or fire pit, where food is slow-cooked all day. Most of this food is of the nonvegetarian variety, you might not be too surprised to learn.

Norway

Norway is the birthplace of the Yule log, traditionally burned at solstice. "Yule" is said to come from the Norse word *hweol*, meaning "wheel." The Norse believed that the sun was a great wheel of fire that rolled toward and then away from the earth (which you have to admit is creative, if scientifically unfounded). In Norway, instead of Santa, the Christmas elf Julnisse brings presents for little girls and boys—but only if they finish all their *lutefisk*, a traditional Norwegian dish made of lye-cured cod. Yes, lye. Yum!

Philippines

Christmas in the Philippines is all about firecrackers (from Christmas Eve until New Year's), which must be a big headache for Filipino fire departments. Decorating and caroling to raise money for church groups (or to get treats for kids) is typical. There are town processions, generally church-sponsored, and Christmas dinner is almost always roast pig.

Pigs have the intelligence of a human three-year-old, just to let you know.

Poland

In Poland, the emphasis is on family togetherness, not gift giving or receiving like it is here in the U.S. On Christmas Eve, everyone watches the sky—not for Santa, but to see the *gwiazdka*, or "little star" (first star of the night), in remembrance of the Star of Bethlehem. After the star is spotted, the Christmas revelry begins, with families settling down to *wigilia*, the meat-free Christmas supper (yes! I'm so moving to Poland), at which it's considered bad luck to have company OR an odd number of people at the table! It's also considered bad luck to leave the table before anyone else. Everyone has to get up at the same time (except for the one empty place at the table left for Baby Jesus).

Portugal

In Portugal, Christmas, or *Natal*, is a huge national celebration. On Christmas Eve, families attend Missa do Galo, Rooster's Mass, and eat fish, with roast chicken reserved for Christmas Day along with *bolo rei*, king cake. Though there isn't much outdoor decorating or many Christmas trees in Portugal, nearly every house has a nativity scene. Santa visits some homes, Baby Jesus others. But either way, good kids get presents. Which is as it should be.

Romania

In Romania, children go from house to house on Christmas Eve, singing carols and reciting ancient legends (um, yawn. I mean, fun). Then everyone goes home for *turta*, a special cake made for Nosterea Domnului Isus, also known as Christmas Eve, which is made up of thin layers of rolled dough to represent the swaddling clothes of the Christ Child (cool). If you've been good, Santa will visit. If not, you get bupkus.

Russia

St. Nicholas is super popular in Russia, and the feast of St. Nicholas, on December 6, is the highlight of the Christmas season for many Russians. Still, it's an old lady named Babouschka who brings gifts for most Russian kids. Russians, as we all know, like marching around, so there are lots of Christmas Eve processions, especially the Krestny Khod procession, which is led by the highest-ranking member of the Russian Orthodox Church. After attending liturgy, Russians go home to Christmas Eve dinner, which features a porridge called *kutya*, eaten from a common dish to symbolize unity. Rumor has it that if a bit of porridge is thrown against the ceiling and sticks, the harvest will be extra bounteous. Rock on, Russia.

Singapore

A former British colony, Singapore is a multicultural society that celebrates the festivals of many countries and religions, and Christmas is definitely one of them. Contests are held to see which hotels and businesses have the nicest Christmas displays, and gift exchanges between friends and colleagues are common. But remember, if you live in Singapore and get gum for Christmas, you have to have a special gum-chewing license to put it in your mouth (this is not a joke. Although if you think about it, it's actually good because all those black spots you see on the sidewalk in New York? Gum. Also birds could eat it and their beaks could get stuck together).

Slovakia

December 6, St. Nicholas (Mikulas) Day, is a big deal in Slovakia, the day when good girls and boys wake up in the morning and find their shoes stuffed with candy (hopefully they remember to look before putting their shoes on). Then on December 13 comes St. Lucy's day. In Slovakia this involves "clearing the houses of evil" by carrying a wooden replica of St. Lucy through the village, then throwing it into

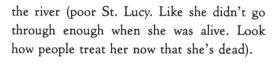

the river (poor St. Lucy. Like she didn't go through enough when she was alive. Look how people treat her now that she's dead).

South Africa

In South Africa, school is closed for Christmas—not for one day, but for FIVE WEEKS, because Christmas falls over South African midsummer. Lucky South Africans. Most families celebrate with an outside meal or *braai*, barbecue, along with swimming or a picnic at the beach. Santa still manages to find his way to South Africa, even though it's summer there in December, and he's probably sweating quite a lot.

Spain

In Spain, Christmas is quite a religious affair, with gifts exchanged on El Día de Reyes, King's Day, or Epiphany, on January 6, instead of on Christmas. And it's the Three Kings or Wise Men who bring good children presents, not Santa. One unusual practice, left over from ancient celebrations of the solstice, still remains, and that's the practice of *hogueras*, bonfires, characterized by people jumping over fires as a symbolic protection against illness (again, the FDNY would NOT approve).

76

Sweden

Christmas Eve is the height of the holiday festivities in Sweden, although St. Lucia Day on December 13 is also huge, since she is the patron saint of Sweden. Lucyfest, or the Festival of Lights, takes place on St. Lucia Day, when it's traditional for the eldest daughter, dressed in a white gown with a crown of candles in her hair (hello, FDNY!) to bring coffee and buns to her parents in the form of breakfast in bed. St. Lucia was a young Christian martyr who was sold into white slavery when she refused to renounce her faith. No one could lift her to carry her to the slave block, though, because God made her so heavy. So then they gouged out her eyes and tried to light her on fire, but her eyes grew back and she wouldn't burn. They also tried to boil her in oil, but she wouldn't boil. Finally, they ran her through with a sword, and that ultimately did the job.

Switzerland

Because Switzerland is such a mountainous country, the various towns there, isolated from one another for many years, each developed their own unique Christmas customs . . . though most of them center on St. Nicholas. Bell ringing, parades, and carol singing all mark the day in various parts of the country. Some other parts of the country, though, might need a little guidance . . . like the town where, on Christmas Eve, young bachelors roam about town behind a sooty rag (or pig's bladder) attached to a pole. In some towns, Christmas traditions such as the pig bladder one got so wild, they were officially moved to New Year's, so as to help people keep in mind Christmas's roots as a holy day. Excuse me, but couldn't these guys just stay home and play *Doom 3* like normal bachelors?

Trinidad and Tobago

Even though they're located in the Caribbean, Santa still finds his way to Trinidad and Tobago (and who can blame him? The weather is a heck of a lot nicer that time of year than it is at the North Pole). The Christmas season on the islands is very festive, with an emphasis on caroling to steel drums and tambourines, known as *parang*, the music of the Caribbean. Christmas dinner may include *pasteles*, beef-filled pastries, and dessert is a special cake soaked in Caribbean rum for several weeks. Sometimes more. Sometimes an extra dash of rum is added to the already rum-soaked cake. I'm just reporting what I've heard.

United Kingdom

They've been celebrating Christmas in the home of the author of *A Christmas Carol* since King Arthur's time, maybe even longer, so they pretty much have it down by now. It's not ENTIRELY about that Christmas pudding Bob Cratchit's family anticipates so eagerly in *A Christmas Carol*, although they're still pretty popular . . . as are Christmas trees, a tradition brought to the British by Queen Victoria's husband, Prince Albert, from his native Germany. Santa Claus, known in England as Father

Christmas, visits overnight on Christmas Eve. Just like in Genovia, the ruling monarch addresses the common people over the airwaves to assure them all is right with the kingdom. And on Boxing Day, the day after Christmas, everyone takes time out to see a pantomime, which can involve large puppets, like the Pantomime Princess Margaret frequently seen on *Monty Python*, a favorite show of Mr. Gianini's for reasons neither my mother nor I can understand.

United States of America

See "Christmas in NYC," page 47, and "Christmas in Indiana," page 55.

Venezuela

On December 16 the Christmas season officially begins in lovely Venezuela, when families bring out their *presebres*,

Nativity scenes, and display them. These *presebres* can sometimes include things not included at the original nativity, such as electric trains, boats, and cartoon figures like Bart Simpson, or action figures like Lara Croft of *Tomb Raider*. Venezuelans are big on imagination and won't be hemmed in by convention. Venezuelan children are left gifts Christmas morning by the Christ Child or Santa. But the good stuff usually comes on January 6, Epiphany, or Day of the Reyes Magos (Three Wise Men), who drop in with candy to signify the end of the Christmas season. Mmmm, candy.

West Africa

Christmas in West Africa is a time when relatives and friends visit one another from town to town—regardless of whether or not they actually celebrate Christmas. Trees are decorated—not necessarily in the home, but in the garden, anyway, and not fir trees, exactly, but native mango or cashew trees. The traditional Christmas Eve dinner consists of a specially cooked rice and goat or chicken stew or soup. Processions and dancing through the streets on Christmas Eve are not unusual, though by Christmas Day everyone has calmed down in time for Father Christmas to show up, bringing chocolate along with the special Akan greeting "Afishapa," meaning "Merry Christmas and Happy New Year," West African style.

CHRISTMAS IN HOLLYWOOD

by Lilly Moscovitz and Mia Thermopolis

Lilly and Mia's Guide to the Top Ten Holiday Movies

Okay, okay, so the holidays are SUPPOSED to be about spending time with family, and not about watching movies.

Well, we discovered a long time ago that a great way to spend time with your family is to spend it WATCHING MOVIES. Yes! That way, there is no fighting—except maybe over which movie to watch.

That's why we've composed this helpful list, so in the future, you won't have to fight—you can just pull out the list, and use it to persuade others of the superiority of your film choice over theirs.

Here goes:

10. *Groundhog Day*
Although technically this a movie that takes place on February 2, or Groundhog Day, it still has a very holidayish feel to it, since it's very funny and uplifting, and is all about living life to its fullest and helping others, which is really what the holidays are all about. Plus, Bill Murray is just hilarious.

9. *The Ref*

Denis Leary plays a thief who gets trapped in a house on Christmas Eve with what is perhaps the most dysfunctional family ever documented on film. As you might expect, this chain-smoking, foul-mouthed criminal knows more about the Christmas spirit than the horrible, supposedly loving family he is trapped with, and ends up teaching them a thing or two about love and family loyalty. Plus, it contains the immortal quote: "Kid. Gag your grandma."

8. *Home for the Holidays*

Jodie Foster directed this hilarious and touching movie about a down-and-out single mom (Holly Hunter) who goes home to visit her parents for Thanksgiving, and ends up alienating her sister, while bonding closer with her gay brother, fabulously played by Robert Downey Jr. (who seems to ad-lib most, if not all, of his lines). Even better? A pre–*The Practice* Dylan McDermott plays Holly Hunter's love interest.

7. *Scrooged*

Another Bill Murray movie, only this one really DOES take place over Christmas. A modern retelling of Charles Dickens's *A Christmas Carol*. In this version, Scrooge is a TV executive who sold his soul (practically) to be rich and famous. Karen Allen stars as the perky social worker he left behind. Carol Kane is hilarious as an abusive Ghost of Christmas Present.

6. *Scrooge* (musical)

This ANCIENT film starring Albert Finney features many songs that you will recognize, such as "Thank You Very Much" and "I Like Life." Well, okay, maybe you won't recognize them, but by the end you'll be humming them. This is by far the best version of *A Christmas Carol* that we know of, plus one of the few with DANCING in it, so that makes it far superior to its nondancing cousins. Plus, it has the best line of any Christmas movie ever: "I want the dolly in the corner!" Say it a few times with an English accent. Go ahead. We DARE you.

5. *It's a Wonderful Life*

This is a fabulous movie about a man who wishes he had never existed and gets his wish (don't worry, it has a happy ending). It's a movie that begs many questions, such as, "Is it possible to watch this movie without crying at the end?" And "How does one spell ZuZu?" And "Why can't Donna Reed be MY mother?" The part when Jimmy Stewart grabs her and says he doesn't want plastics is actually way hot, for a Christmas movie.

4. *The Santa Clause*

We hate to admit it, but this movie is a bit of a guilty pleasure, enjoyable even if you AREN'T seven years old. Tim Allen plays a man who inherits the role of Santa—the REAL Santa—and is none too pleased about porking out and having to move to the North Pole . . . though his son couldn't be more delighted. This movie answers a lot of those questions that have bothered us, such as, "How does Santa get to every house in one night?" And "Does he really eat all those cookies?" Satisfying as Oreos and a glass of milk.

3. *Die Hard*

A lot of people forget this is a Christmas movie, but that's the whole reason Bruce Willis is visiting his wife in the first place. See, she moved to L.A. for a fancy new job, while her husband stayed in New York to be a cop. So he's coming home for the holidays to patch things up, and—as usually happens—Eurotrash terrorists choose Christmas Eve to take everyone in his wife's office hostage. Bruce has to save the day . . . and not to give anything away, but he survives to make *Die Hard 2*.

2. *National Lampoon's Christmas Vacation*

This movie is the silly antidote to all the sappy Suzanne Somers made-for-TV holiday movies you've been watching (don't even try to deny it). Chevy Chase doesn't get the Christmas bonus he'd counted on receiving in order to build his family a pool, and he goes a little insane. But you can understand why after you meet his in-laws. Not to mention the squirrel in the Christmas tree.

And the number one Christmas movie of all time . . .

1. *A Christmas Story*

This movie is written by a guy from Indiana, and also set there, but the story of his main character, Ralphie's, obsession with owning a Red Ryder air rifle is familiar to us all, Hoosier or not (only for Mia it was Prom Dress Barbie. For Lilly, an electromagnetic microscope). Ralphie's endeavors to be good so he can earn his rifle—his fantasies about what he'll do when he gets his rifle—his painful trip to see Santa to ask for the rifle—and his adventures along the way—all speak to the heart of what Christmas is all about in the eyes of a child. Speaking of eyes, the best line in the whole movie? "Yellow eyes! He had yellow eyes!" Hasn't every kid in the world been menaced by a yellow-eyed bully? What's UP with that???

V

Xmas
Xtras

Just like you can never have enough wrapping paper, you can never have enough Christmas.

Well, okay, maybe you can. Like after you've eaten the entire contents of your Christmas stocking AND the candy canes off the tree AND watched *The Little Drummer Boy* seventeen times in a row. Not that I've ever done this.

More than once a year, anyway.

ADVENT

by Grandmère, Dowager Princess of Genovia

Somebody Bring Me a Sidecar

Advent takes place during the period beginning the Sunday closest to the feast of St. Andrew, and ending Christmas Day. It is thought that the four weeks of Advent symbolize the four thousand years of darkness in which the world was enveloped before the birth of Jesus Christ, although there is no liturgical confirmation of this of which I am aware.

Advent is a time of preparation for the anniversary of the Lord's coming on December 25. Many might confuse this with Yule, which has its roots in pagan worship. Nothing could be further from the truth. Although it is true that by the time Advent arrives, there are very few shopping days for Christmas left, and when Yule arrives, there are even FEWER, and one might as well just give up all hope of using anything but Overnight Express if you want it to get there in time for Christmas.

[So true.]

{*Princess Party Tip:*
You don't have to own a calendar made by Fabergé in the shape of the Genovian palace (with windows that really open

to reveal a jewel inside to represent each of the days of Advent) to celebrate the four weeks of Advent. You can make your own Advent calendar! To do so, you will need:

- Big piece of felt
- Another piece of felt
- Glue
- Scissors
- Fabric marker

Cut out one big piece of felt. Then cut out twenty-five smaller pieces of felt (approximately the size and shape of playing cards). Glue the sides and bottoms of the smaller pieces of felt in five rows of five each across the big piece of felt, leaving the tops open.

After numbering the pockets you've created for the days of Advent with the fabric marker, fill the twenty-five pockets with something of your choice—clues to a scavenger hunt around the house, leading to a small prize; nuts or hard candies; money; slips of paper with lyrics from Christmas carols or a Biblical quote written on them; video game tokens; pieces of a puzzle.

Starting on December 1, each day, pull one object from the pocket corresponding to that day, until you reach December 25. Fun for the whole family!

Enjoy!}

THE CHRISTMAS TREE

by Helen Thermopolis,
celebrated painter and mother of Princess Mia

Dead Celebrities Get Their Due

Is there anything that lifts the spirits more than the sight of a Christmas tree? Even people in ancient times hung evergreens around their peat-moss huts in order to remind themselves that spring, a time when everything turns green again, was around the corner.

Is it any wonder the tradition stuck?

Druids were among the first to place fir trees in their homes in the dead of winter as a symbol of everlasting life. Martin Luther, a founder of the Protestant faith, is said to be the first to have the idea of decorating his fir tree, an idea that came to him as he walked through the woods one night and noticed how shiny the ice crystals hanging from the branches were in the moonlight. So he placed candles on the ends of each branch of his own tree indoors to repli cate the glistening icicles he'd seen.

[Today, this effect is much more economically—and safely—accomplished with twinkly lights and/or tinsel. The use of open flames any-

where near evergreens is frowned upon by the New York Fire Department.]

While the Christmas tree in the Genovian palace might sparkle with lovely bejeweled and priceless ornaments, I have always found that the most beautiful—and meaningful—decorations are those made by the hands of friends or family members, because those decorations are made with the rarest jewel of all—love.

{*Princess Party Tip:*

Do what my mom does every year, and pay homage to The Year That Was: Decorate YOUR tree with the images of celebrities who have died during the course of the previous year.

All you need to make your own Dead Celebrity Tree is:
- A tree
- Magazines
- Scissors
- Glue
- Cardboard
- Yarn

Look through magazines for images of dead celebrities. When you find one you like, cut it out. Glue it to some cardboard. Trim the cardboard. Poke a hole through the top. Tie it to a branch with yarn. *Voilà!* Your own Dead Celebrity Tree.

Enjoy!}

THE CAROLS

by Boris Pelkowski, musical genius and mouth breather

Good King Wenceslas, Victim of Fratricide

Throughout history, music has always played an important part in any celebration. We sing and play instruments to express our greatest joys (and sometimes sorrows). Our earliest ancestors realized this, and that's why many of our most beloved Christmas carols actually got their start as age-old chants or hymns, folk songs created by simple peasants, since singing in the church was forbidden for many years.

It was St. Francis of Assisi who recognized the importance of song in celebration of life, and who brought these folk songs into the formal worship of the church during a Christmas midnight mass in a cave in Greccio, in the province of Umbria, in 1223. These songs were then spread across the land by wandering minstrels who traveled from hamlet to castle, performing them in exchange for alms (money).

In a time when few people knew how to read (and even fewer books were actually printed) song was an important teaching tool. The popular carol, "Good King Wenceslas," actually memorializes a real historical figure, a Bohemian

king who was murdered in A.D. 929 by his own brother (and whose mother murdered his grandmother. You might say it ran in the family.). Through song, the memory of Wenceslas lived on, teaching his lesson of being kind to one's neighbors.

Today, many people still go caroling in order to spread holiday cheer and joy. I hope, however, that they don't get their hopes up about getting any alms, because the last time

I went caroling, all I got was a few pennies and a piece of raisin bread. Although that might have been because I was playing Bartók. But still.

[I know. You've heard "Jingle Bell Rock" so many times, you're ready to rip off your own ears. But here are some Christmas selections you won't get tired of (at least, not right away):

- *Mr. Hankey's Christmas Classics* (*South Park*)
- *Punk Rock Christmas* (various artists/punk)
- *You Sleigh Me* (various artists/alternative)
- *Christmas with the Rat Pack* (Frank Sinatra, Sammy Davis Jr., Dean Martin)
- *My Kind of Christmas* (Christina Aguilera)

And don't be dissing Xtina, she's got, like, a seven-octave range, for God's sake.

And don't forget the Muppets and *A Charlie Brown Christmas*, for those times you're feeling insanely 70s.]

{*Princess Party Tip:*
If carolers show up at your house or apartment, don't be a grinch! It's polite to offer them a small donation if they are caroling for charity, or at least a warm drink. Bringing them a figgy pudding isn't necessary, but remember the "we won't go until we get some" line. Better safe than sorry.}

THE TRUTH ABOUT ST. NICK,

*aka Santa Claus, Kris Kringle, Christkindl,
Père Noël, Saint Nicholas, Papa Noel, Father Christmas,
Old Man Christmas, Santa Kurohsu*

by Artur Phillipe Renaldo, Prince of Genovia

Many people assume (erroneously) that Saint Nicholas (Sinterklaas or Santa Claus) was a fat, jolly man who achieved immortality and currently lives at the North Pole with his wife and some reindeer.

Nothing could be farther from the truth. A powerful bishop who at one time was thrown into prison, Nicholas of Myra, believed strongly in helping young people (particularly young brides in need of a dowry). He was like a one-man scholarship fund, often dropping bags of gold anonymously down the chimney when he knew certain young ladies' fathers did not approve of their matches.

Because of this generosity, Nicholas was declared a saint . . . but like many popular leaders, he was not allowed to rest, even after his death. His remains were said to have miraculous healing properties, and so were eventually stolen from his tomb in his native land, which is why today they are stored in the beautiful Basilica of Saint Nicholas.

[EW!!! THEY TOUCHED HIS BONES!!!!]

During the Reformation, attempts to make people forget about Saint Nicholas were unsuccessful—as attempts to make anyone forget the kindnesses of a past ruler often are. But the people could never forget such a kind and thoughtful regent. Nicholas was reborn in the guise of the "Christkindl" (Christ child, later shortened to Kris Kringle), who placed nuts and candies in the shoes of children who had been good throughout the year. Good behavior on the part of children has been rewarded by parents, in the guise of St. Nicholas, for centuries ever since . . . much in the way that productive members of society receive a tax refund from the government at the end of the year, except in Genovia where, of course, there are no taxes, due to the benefaction of a certain current regent.

Modern-day Santa probably came from an illustration in an 1870 edition of *A Visit from Saint Nicholas*, in which Saint Nicholas is depicted wearing a red cloth coat. This image has, of course, been reinforced by hundreds of thousands of illustrations ever since, but probably has absolutely no relation to how the real Nicholas looked or dressed—much in the way the image of me, on the currency of Genovia, bears no real likeness to how I appear today, since shaving my mustache.

[Um, and losing all your hair. And let us not forget what is probably the most enduring image of Santa to American children: the scary shopping mall Santa, whose lap we are required to sit on. Why do these Santas always smell funny? And why did he never bring me the Prom Dress Barbie I wanted?]

THE CHRISTMAS STAR

*by Kenny Showalter, conspiracy theorist
and Biology lab partner of Princess Mia*

White Dwarf or Jupiter in Retrograde?

While many assume the Star of Bethlehem was only a myth, some of us disagree. Some of us, in fact, have spent many, many hours analyzing data from the numerous astronomical events around the time of Jesus's birth that could have provided the star the Three Wise Men (aka Magi, or astrologers, as some New Testament translations explicitly call them—later translations bumped them up to "king" status) followed to Bethlehem.

Our research has led to some startling theories that could, should they become more widely known, shake the foundations of Santaland as we know it:

CONJUNCTION: There were three extremely rare conjunctions (a conjunction is when two or more objects appear very close together in the sky) of planets around the time of Jesus's birth—one in May, when the Wise Men would have started out on their journey, the second in late September, when they were visiting King Herod, and the third in early December, over Bethlehem, when they would have been leaving Herod's palace. Though Jupiter and Saturn never got close enough together to be confused as a single object, the word for "star" may have had a different definition than it does today. WAS IT A CONJUNCTION THE WISE MEN SAW????

NOVA: While the exact time of Jesus's birth is not known, Chinese astronomers recorded a new star (nova) in the constellation Capricorn around the time He was thought to have been born. This star was said to have been visible for more than two months. Novas are caused by dying stars (so the term "new star" is erroneous, as they are actually very old stars), which sometimes become white dwarves, due to thermonuclear reactions on the surface as the stars die, which flare very bright, then fade from view in a few months. Possibly, it was a nova the Wise Men were following.

METEOR, SHOOTING STAR, COMET: A meteor lasts only a few seconds or minutes at best. The Wise Men followed the star for weeks looking for Jesus, so it couldn't have been a shooting star. We can rule out comets for the same reason. A comet is not stationary long enough for the Wise Men to have followed it for as long as they did, therefore ruling out this theory (HA! I TOLD you shooting star theorists that your idea was lame!).

JUPITER IN RETROGRADE: Many astronomers feel the star was simply Jupiter undergoing retrograde motion (going backwards; stars do this sometimes, the same way I sometimes put my shirts on backward and don't realize it until I get to school). While in retrograde, the planet appears to be stationary for about a week. Jupiter in retrograde, while ALSO in a conjunction with other planets (see first theory), would have been the brightest point in the sky, besides the moon, at that time, and COULD be the star the Wise Men were following.

The above are just SOME of the many, many theories out there that could explain the Star of Bethlehem. Could there be other, as yet unexplored, explanations? Oh, yes, my friend. And while some people suggest it's better not to examine the science behind historical miracles, as the findings can be disappointing, I, however, disagree, at least so far as the Christmas star is concerned. To me, as to the ancients who recorded its viewing, the star symbolizes hope—and isn't that what Christmas is all about?

[That is so sweet, Kenny! But, I'm sorry, you'd better not be hoping that I'm going to the Nondenominational Winter Dance with you.]

103

celebrating

Kwanzaa

A Note from
Her Royal Highness Princess Mia

There aren't many holidays that were invented by an actual person, as opposed to a group of people, like the Maccabees or Romans. That isn't true about Kwanzaa, though, because it was invented by Dr. Maulana Karenga. When I take over the throne of Genovia, one of the first things I'm going to do is invent my own holiday. It's going to be called Mia Day, and on Mia Day, everybody has to go to their local animal shelter and adopt a pet.

Unless they have a cat like Fat Louie at home, who might shred any other pet in his vicinity to pieces. Then they can just go to the animal shelter and take a stray dog for a walk and then return him later, or something. Because I don't want to cause any peticides.

THREE CHEERS FOR KWANZAA

by Shameeka Taylor, AEHS cheerleader

Kwanzaa is another midwinter celebration like Christmas or Hanukkah, only Kwanzaa doesn't have a religious basis. Instead, it's a unique African-American celebration that focuses on the traditional African values of family, community responsibility, commerce, and self-improvement. It's a time for people, especially African Americans, to reaffirm their culture and ancestral heritage.

Kwanzaa is based on the *nguzo saba* (seven guiding principles), one for each day of the observance, and is celebrated from December 26 to January 1. Because the names of the days of Kwanzaa are in the African language of Kiswahili, I created a cheer about them, since they can sometimes be difficult to remember. Just shout the word and its meaning in a very loud voice, preferably while jumping up and down with pom-poms:

Umoja (OO-MO-JAH)   —Unity!
Kujichagulia (KOO-JEE-CHA-GOO-LEE-YAH)
                          —Self-determination!
Ujima (OO-JEE-MAH)   —Responsibility!
Ujamaa (OO-JAH-MAH)   —Cooperation!
Nia (NEE-YAH)   —Purpose!

Kuumba (KOO-OOM-BAH) —Creativity!
Imani (EE-MAH-NEE)   —Faith!

Don't worry if the neighbors ask you to keep it down. Just tell them you're celebrating Kwanzaa, which they will probably know anyway because your home will be decorated in the colors of Kwanzaa (black, red, and green).

[What about the gifts? Aren't there PRESENTS?]

It is traditional to give creative or artistic gifts—preferably homemade—on the last day of Kwanzaa, January 1.

[In other words, a Segway Human Transporter would not be an appropriate Kwanzaa gift.]

Ready? Okay!
KWANZAA YENU IWE NA HERI! (HAPPY KWANZAA!)

{*Princess Party Tip:*
Hold your own Kwanzaa Karumu (the Kwanzaa feast traditionally held on December 31)! A typical Kwanzaa menu should include traditional African dishes such as peanut soup, chicken stew, sweet potato fritters, couscous, and fried plantains. A fun recipe you can try at home is benne cakes. Benne (which means "sesame seed") cakes are from West Africa, where sesame seeds are eaten for good luck.

To make benne cakes, grease a cookie sheet with oil and preheat your oven to 325 degrees. Then gather up:

1 cup firmly packed brown sugar
1/4 cup softened butter or margarine
1 egg, beaten
1/2 teaspoon vanilla extract
1/2 teaspoon freshly squeezed lemon juice

½ cup all-purpose flour
½ teaspoon baking powder
¼ teaspoon salt
1 cup toasted sesame seeds

Mix together the brown sugar and butter, and beat until they are creamy. Stir in the egg, vanilla extract, and lemon juice. Add flour, baking powder, salt, and sesame seeds. Drop by rounded teaspoons onto the cookie sheet two inches apart. Bake for 15 minutes or until the edges are browned. Makes about 2 dozen cakes.

Enjoy!}

VII

HAPPY NEW YEAR

A Note from
Her Royal Highness Princess Mia

As everyone knows, New Year's Day is the day marking the end of the previous year's calendar, and the beginning of a new one. This is one of the most ancient of all the holidays, beginning in Babylon about four THOUSAND years ago.

Of course, back then they didn't have Times Square to drop the ball in, or even Dick Clark, so the Babylonians celebrated by slaughtering a bunch of innocent animals and eating them. Probably a few virgins, too.

Slaughtering them, I mean. Not eating them.

Most cultures held their New Year's festivities on the spring solstice—a sign that winter was over, and a new agricultural season was beginning. A lot of the New Year's traditions we practice today are the same ones practiced by the ancient civilizations before us. Who knew making a New Year's resolution—such as not biting your fingernails anymore—is actually very Babylonian? I had no idea I was so cosmopolitan!

BABY NEW YEAR

by Rocky Thermopolis Gianini,
baby brother of Princess Mia

Call Child Protective Services!

Goo goo gee mwah fa la la la, twee goo.

[Since Rocky is still a baby and can't speak English properly, I will translate. Here he is saying: The tradition of using a baby to symbolize the new year is actually Greek. It was traditional in 600 B.C. to parade around on New Year's Day with a baby in a basket. The baby was supposed to be Dionysus, the god of wine, reborn for the new year.

I would just like to say that this was a very irresponsible way to treat a baby. I hope those baskets had safety belts.]

Gew! Gwah ma dee lo FO!

[Here Rocky is saying that the Greeks weren't the only ones who used a baby to represent rebirth. The Egyptians did it too.

This was very irresponsible of them, as well.]

Dum do dee fwah goo.

[Rocky says the tradition of using a baby to represent the birth of a new year carried on through countless generations until it reached today's greeting card industry, which has used it almost to death. Thank you, Rocky, for your keen insight into this horrible abuse of babies throughout history.]

Goo!

[Rocky says, "You're welcome!"]

NEW YEAR'S KISS

by Tina Hakim Baba, romance expert

When Harry Frenched Sally

Everyone who's seen the movie *When Harry Met Sally* knows how vitally important it is that you kiss someone special at the stroke of midnight on New Year's Eve.

But does everyone know WHY it's so important?

Traditionally, it's always been thought that what a person does on the first day of the year will affect his or her luck throughout the REST of that year. To this day, many people throughout the world believe that if you eat a certain food—donuts in Denmark, ham or black-eyed peas in the southern U.S., cabbage or rice elsewhere—you will have luck in the new year.

In olden times, some cultures believed that if their first visitor of the year was a tall, dark-haired man, they would have good luck. It is no mystery why so many heroes in romance novels are tall, dark, and handsome! For centuries, tall, dark, and handsome men have been considered sought-after houseguests on New Year's Day.

Kissing someone you love romantically on

the stroke of midnight on New Year's Eve is also considered lucky, and bodes well for the health of your relationship. Kissing a boy on New Year's Eve, however, doesn't necessarily mean you will still be with that boy on the FOLLOWING New Year's.

But it's definitely a start!

AULD LANG SYNE

by Boris Pelkowksi, musical genius and mouth breather

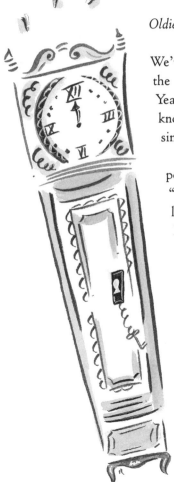

Oldie But Goodie

We've all heard party guests singing the song "Auld Lang Syne" at New Year's. But does anyone actually know what it means, or why people sing it?

At least partially written by the poet Robert Burns in the 1700s, "Auld Lang Syne" was first published after Burns's death in 1796. But the song actually has its roots much earlier than 1700. Robert Burns just came up with the modern rendition. *Auld lang syne* is Scottish for "old long ago," or simply, "the good old days." When people sing it, they are saying, "Don't forget the good times we had in Gifted and Talented class," or something similar.

The actual words are:

Should auld acquaintance be forgot
   and never brought to mind?
Should auld acquaintance be forgot
   and days of auld lang syne?
For auld lang syne, my dear,
   for auld lang syne,
We'll take a cup of kindness yet,
   for auld lang syne.

[This is not unlike the Girl Scout song, "Make new friends, but keep the old, one is silver, the other is gold." Which is how I feel about Lilly and Tina. Not that any of us were ever Girl Scouts, due to no one's mom ever wanting to be the troop leader.]

New Year's Resolutions

1.
2.
3.
4.
5.
6.

RESOLUTIONS

Doom 3 *Is an Excellent Game*

*by Michael Moscovitz,
Royal Consort to the
Princess of Genovia*

People have been making New Year's resolutions for approximately four thousand years. The first to do so were the Babylonians, who used the new year as a reminder to return their neighbors' farm equipment.

Today's resolutions are generally more personal in nature, from resolving to lose weight or get in shape, quit smoking, give up junk food, or spend less time playing *Doom 3* and more quality time with your girlfriend.

Although, if your girlfriend would just take the time to learn how to play *Doom 3*, the two of you could play it TOGETHER, and spend more quality time with each other while at the same time fighting off the massive demonic invasion that has overwhelmed the Union Aerospace Corporation (UAC) Mars Research Facility, leaving chaos and horror in its wake, of which you are one of the few survivors. . . .

[I am not learning how to play that game, okay??? It's stupid and boring! And there are no girls in it!]

Actually, there are girls in it, if you would just—

[I'll tell you what: I'll play *Doom 3* with you if you'll play *Dance Dance Revolution Party* with me.]

As I was saying, New Year's is the perfect time to amend behaviors or traits that might be keeping you from becoming the fully self-actualized individual you have always yearned to be. Don't let the fact that researchers say most people abandon their New Year's resolutions less than three weeks after January 1 stop you. Record your resolutions here as a reminder to yourself.

[And let go of that joystick!]

My New Year's Resolutions

I resolve in the new year to: _____

_____

_____

_____

_____

_____

_____

HOW TO SAY "HAPPY NEW YEAR" AROUND THE GLOBE

by Grandmère, Dowager Princess of Genovia

Learn This or Else

A princess knows that good manners are a MUST whilst entertaining. Nothing breaks the ice at a peace summit or cocktail party faster than greeting someone in his or her native language. With the following guide, you will be able to wish anyone, from a backpacking tourist or a foreign ambassador, Happy New Year with culture and panache. Start memorizing, please:

Afghani	Saale Nao Mubbarak
Afrikaans	Voorspoedige Nuwejaar
Albanian	Gëzuar Vitin e Ri
Arabic	Kull'aam wa-antum bikhayr
Bengali	Shuvo Nabo Borsho
Bulgarian	Chestita Nova Godina
Chinese (Mandarin)	Kong He Xin Xi
Corsican	Bon dì, bon'annu

Croatian	Sretna Nova Godina
Cymraeg (Welsh)	Blwyddyn Newydd Dda
Czechoslovakia	Stastny Novy Rok
Danish	Godt Nytår
Dutch	Gelukkig Nieuwjaar
Eskimo (Aleut)	Amlertut Kiaget
Estonian	Hääd uut aastat
Finnish	Onnellista Uutta Vuotta
French	Bonne Année
German	Ein glückliches neues Jahr
Greek	Kalón étos eisélthois
Hawaiian	Hauloi Makahiki Hou
Hebrew	L'Shanah Tovah
Hindi	Nahi varsh ki haardik shubh kaamnaayen
Hungarian	Boldog új évet
Indonesian	Selamat Tahun Baru
Iraqi	Sanah Jadidah
Irish (Gaelic)	Bhliain nua fe nhaise dhuit
Italian	Felice Anno Nuovo

Japanese	Akimashite omedetou gozaimasu
Kannada	Hosa Varushadha Shubhashayagalu
Kisii	Somwaka Omoyia Omuya
Khmer	Sua Sdei tfnam tmei
Lao	Sabai dee pee mai
Malay	Selamat Tahun Baru
Maltese	Is Sena T-Tajba
Nepali	Nawa Barsha ko Hardik Shuvakamana
Norwegian	Godt Nytt År
Papua New Guinean	Nupela yia i go long yu
Philippine (Tagalog)	Maligayang Bagong Taon
Polish	Szczesliwego Nowego Roku
Portuguese	Feliz Ano Novo
Punjabi	Namae Saaldiyan Mubarakan
Romanian	La Mulit Ani
Russian	S Novyim Godom
Serbo-Croatian	Srečna Nova Godina
Sindhi	Nayou Saal Mubbarak Hoje

Singhalese	Subha Aluth Awrudhak Vewa
Slovak	Stastlivy Novy Rok
Somali	Iyo Sanad Cusub Oo Fiican
Spanish	Feliz Año Nuevo
Swahili	Karibu Mwaka Mupia
Swedish	Gott Nytt Ár
Sudanese	Warsa Enggal
Tamil	Pudhu Varusha Vaazthukkal
Telegu	Noothana samvatsara shubhakankshalu
Thai	Sawadee Pii Mai
Turkish	Yeni Iyi Senele
Ukrainian	Z Novim Rokom
Urdu	Naya Saal Mubarak Ho
Uzbek	Yangi Yil Bilan
Vietnamese	Chúc Mùng Nam Mói

VIII

So I have traditionally spent New Year's Eve at my friend Lilly's apartment, generally viewing either a James Bond, Arnold Schwarzenegger, or *Die Hard* movie marathon, and making our own ice cream creations, such as Times Square Éclair (Twinkies stuffed with vanilla ice cream and sprinkled with red, white, and blue nonpareils) or Dick Clark Clark Bars (ice cream with Clark bars crumbled over it, then refrozen in various shapes, some of them quite phallic).

Most often, I wake on the morning of New Year's Day with a feeling that I've forgotten something . . . and then I remember:

My teeth. I never brushed them the night before. Ew. Clark Bar plaque.

But other cultures, such as the Chinese, celebrate the New Year in a very different fashion . . . and not even, it turns out, on the same night every year. And there's not a Clark Bar to be seen . . .

WHAT'S YOUR SIGN?

An Interview between Princess Mia and
Ling Su Wong, blossoming artist and Chinese American

Mia: Ling Su, I am very interested in Chinese New Year. What can you tell me about it?

Ling Su: Well, Mia, Chinese New Year is different than Western New Year—it falls on a different day every year since the Chinese calendar is based on astronomical observations of the movement of the sun, stars, and the lunar cycle, making it the longest chronological record in history, and actually more accurate than the Western calendar, which is kind of random on account of different world leaders or popes sticking days in here and there throughout history.

Chinese New Year starts with the new moon on the first day of the new year and ends on the full moon fifteen days later.

Mia: Is this when you light off the firecrackers?

Ling Su: Chinese New Year may seem to Westerners to be about lighting firecrackers, since a lot of that goes on in

Chinatown during our New Year celebration. However, Chinese New Year is really about celebrating the coming of spring, as well as uniting living relatives with those relatives who have passed away—in other words, honoring our ancestors. A feast is prepared in remembrance of those ancestors who have left us, often with place settings left empty for them.

Mia: So when do you set off the firecrackers?

Ling Su: Firecrackers are lit for a number of reasons. Nobody really knows which one is the real one. One reason may be that the noise supposedly wakes up the dragon who brings the spring rain for the crops. Another belief is that the sound of the fireworks is supposed to scare away all evil spirits and misfortunes. In this way, evil will be prevented from coming into the new year.

Mia: What about all those little red envelopes I see lying around Chinatown after New Year's?

Ling Su: They are part of an old custom called *hong bao* "red packet," in which married couples and the elderly give money in red envelopes (the color red is known to ward away evil) to children for luck in the new year.

Mia: This sounds like a very excellent custom that should be incorporated here in the U.S.

Ling Su: Totally. I raked it in last year.

Anyway, the Chinese don't just have their own special New Year's. They also have their own zodiac, different from the one known to the Western world. Instead of being based on the constellations or the twelve months of the year, the Chinese zodiac is based on a twelve-YEAR cycle. This is on account of Buddha. The way the story goes is, when Buddha called all the animals of China to his bedside, only twelve came. Because he wanted to honor the animals for their devotion, he created a year for each animal. The twelve animals that showed up at Buddha's side were the rat, ox, tiger, rabbit, dragon, snake, horse, sheep, monkey, rooster, dog, and pig.

Each of these animals, as you probably know, has its own special characteristics—but they may not be the characteristics you'd expect from that animal. Many Chinese people believe that individuals born into a certain year will grow up to have qualities and personality traits of that year's animal.

Mia: No way! That is SO cool. So I could be a Taurus AND something else? Show me!

Ling Su: Here's a chart. Find the year of your birth, then the animal that corresponds to that year. Remember that Chinese New Year doesn't fall on January 1—so if you were born in February, you might actually fall under the

PREVIOUS year's sign, depending on when Chinese New Year fell that year.

1948, 1960, 1972, 1984, 1996, 2008—Year of the Rat
The rat is charming, bright, creative, and thrifty.
Best love match: Horse
Famous rats: Gwyneth Paltrow, Eminem, Ben Affleck, Prince Harry

1949, 1961, 1973, 1985, 1997, 2009—Year of the Ox
The ox is steadfast, dependable, and methodical.
Best love match: Snake
Famous oxen: Neve Campbell, Zac Hanson, Meg Ryan, Walt Disney

1950, 1962, 1974, 1986, 1998, 2010—Year of the Tiger
The tiger is dynamic, warm, sincere, and a leader.
Best love match: Horse
Famous tigers: Jodie Foster, Tom Cruise, Ryan Phillipe, Mary-Kate and Ashley Olsen

1951, 1963, 1975, 1987, 1999, 2011—Year of the Rabbit
The rabbit is humble, artistic, long-lived, and clear-sighted.
Best love match: Pig
Famous rabbits: Drew Barrymore,

Brad Pitt, Tobey Maguire, Albert Einstein,
Robin Williams

1952, 1964, 1976, 1988, 2000, 2012—Year of the Dragon
The dragon is flamboyant, lucky, and imaginative.
Best love match: Dog
Famous dragons: Sandra Bullock, J.C. Chasez,
Freddie Prinze Jr., Martin Luther King Jr.

1953, 1965, 1977, 1989, 2001, 2013—Year of the Snake
The snake is discreet, refined, and intelligent.
Best love match: Rooster
Famous snakes: Sarah Michelle Gellar, Shakira,
Sarah Jessica Parker, Abraham Lincoln, Oprah Winfrey

1954, 1966, 1978, 1990, 2002, 2014—
Year of the Horse
The horse is social, down to earth, and
appealing to others.
Best love match: Dog
Famous horses: Cindy Crawford, Meg
Cabot, Harrison Ford, Halle Berry

1955, 1967, 1979, 1991, 2003, 2015—
Year of the Sheep/Goat
The sheep/goat is artistic, fastidious,
caring, and forgiving.
Best love match: Pig

Famous sheep/goats: Matt LeBlanc,
Claire Danes, Julia Roberts, Michelangelo

1956, 1968, 1980, 1992, 2004, 2016—Year of the Monkey
The monkey is witty, popular, good-humored, and
versatile.
Best love match: Rat
Famous monkeys: Christina Aguilera, Justin Timberlake,
Will Smith, Charles Dickens

1957, 1969, 1981, 1993, 2005, 2017—Year of the Rooster
The rooster is attractive, aggressive, alert, and a
perfectionist.
Best love match: Snake
Famous roosters: Britney Spears, Jennifer Aniston,
Confucius

1958, 1970, 1982, 1994, 2006, 2018—Year of the Dog
The dog is honest, conservative, sympathetic, and loyal.
Best love match: Horse
Famous dogs: Madonna, Prince William, Jennifer Lopez,
Uma Thurman

1959, 1971, 1983, 1995, 2007,
2019—Year of the Pig
The pig is popular, caring, industri-
ous, and home-loving.
Best love match: Sheep/Goat

Famous pigs: Luke Wilson, Julie Andrews, Stephen King, Ewan McGregor, Elton John

Mia: Chinese New Year is so cool! I wish I could celebrate it!

Ling Su: You can! Clip out the image of the dragon below, attach to your coat, and go!

Mia: Don't forget to light your firecrackers WELL AWAY from your face!

Conclusion

A Note from
Her Royal Highness Princess Mia

As you can see, the winter holiday season is just JAM-PACKED with history, tradition, and festivities. Who knew the origin of the dreidel was from medieval England, or that St. Nicholas's bones once got stolen, or that people used to "Deck the Halls" with boughs of holly in order to look pagan in front of Roman soldiers? Not me.

Personally, I'm glad I learned all this stuff. Because now when I travel to foreign lands—or even just down to Chinatown—I will actually have some idea what people are talking about when they mention Julnisse or even *hong bao*.

More important, however, I'll know that holidays like Christmas, New Year's Day, Hanukkah, and Kwanzaa—different as they may seem from one another—all have one thing in common. And no, it's not presents. It's that they all celebrate birth—rebirth of spring, birth of a savior, birth of hope—and a time of coming together as families and communities to give thanks for that big wheel in the sky rolling toward us once again.

God bless us, everyone.

Now pass me my presents, please.

MEG CABOT is the author of the bestselling, critically acclaimed Princess Diaries books, which were made into the wildly popular Disney movies of the same name. Her other books for teens include ALL-AMERICAN GIRL, READY OR NOT, TEEN IDOL, the Mediator series, NICOLA AND THE VISCOUNT and VICTORIA AND THE ROGUE. Meg divides her time between New York City and Key West with her royal consort and a one-eyed cat named Henrietta. Even though she spends the winter holidays in Florida, she still misses snow. A little.

CHESLEY McLAREN's work has graced the pages and windows of such fashionable clients as *Vogue*, *Instyle*, *The New York Times*, Saks Fifth Avenue, and Bergdorf Goodman. She debuted as an author/illustrator with ZAT CAT!, A HAUTE COUTURE TAIL and illustrated YOU FORGOT YOUR SKIRT, AMELIA BLOOMER! Chesley spends Christmas in Manhattan, where she lives with her royal consort and a two-eyed cat, Monsieur Etoile. She loves the magnificent tree at Rockefeller Center, the shop windows, and especially the wonderful scent of the Christmas trees on all the street corners. In fact, the only thing she does not love about Christmas is being too grown-up to get a stocking from Santa!